God goes to church

Enjoy God! ☺

EdWiNA GaTeLeY

Edwina

SOURCE BOOKS   TRABUCO CANYON   CALIFORNIA

PAX CHRISTI USA PUBLICATIONS   ERIE   PENNSYLVANIA

To
the children, women and men
of the New Faith Community, Rochester, New York,
whose courage and vision has created
a new way of being Church

One rainy day, God was sitting in heaven reading a special book which people had written all about Him.

God came to the bit where it said that people should pray and worship on a certain day called Sunday or the *Sabbath.*

God suddenly had a great idea! God wanted to see what all the people did in those special places at special times. So God called Stardrop, one of His fun-loving angels.
'Let's go to Earth and check it out!' said God.

'Yipeee!' yelled Stardrop.

'Don't you think the people will get worried when we show up?' said Stardrop.
'We'll be very quiet and we'll *whisper,*' said God.
'Quiet as a mouse?' asked Stardrop.
'Quiet as a mouse,' said God.
'And we could even be invisible!' said Stardrop.

So they packed a few things for the journey:

2 fat cushions to sit on
3 boxes of crispy crackers
4 chunks of cheese
5 bars of chocolate
6 apples from the garden
and a large umbrella in case it rained.

Down they flew

And there waiting to meet them was
Chester the Church Mouse with his wagon.

'Great to see you, God and Stardrop!'
squeaked Chester. 'I'll show you around.'
Chester volunteered to carry the cheese,
and off they went...

First they went into an ordinary-looking building where everyone sat very still and very quiet. Nobody said a word.

'When are they going to say something?' asked God.

'Ssshh! They don't talk here,' said Chester.

'Gadzooks!' said God.

And they flew off to find another church.

Next day they went into a church where everyone looked very happy and sang loud and lots and lots of loud songs.

'When are they going to be quiet so they can listen to the music in their hearts?' whispered God. 'They don't believe in their own music,' answered Chester. 'Gadzooks!' said God.

And they flew off to find another church.

After they had eaten some chocolate and an apple and got drenched with rain, God and Stardrop and Chester went into a very fine looking church where special smoke called incense filled the air and lots of little bells were rung. Everyone at the front was dressed in the most beautiful gold clothes and tall, funny shaped hats.

'Why are they all dressed up like that and looking so sad and serious?' whispered God 'Cos they think *You're* very strict!' answered Chester. 'Gadzooks!' said God.

And they flew off to find another church.

wet...
wet....

The next church was loads and loads of fun. People were hugging each other and dancing around. The music was loud and lively.

After the people had stopped hugging and dancing, they lined up to go to the front to share communion bread. But a few people stayed at the back.

'Why doesn't everyone get to go up?' asked God.
'Cos not everyone is allowed,' answered Chester.
'Gadzooks!' said God.

And they flew off to find another church.

Shame.

Next, God decided to be a lady God (because God can do and be anything) and Chester took them all to a big church called a Cathedral. A line of men dressed in long robes and sashes went up to the front.

'Where are all the ladies?'
whispered God.
'They don't have ladies here,'
answered Chester, 'because they
think you are a *man!*'
'Gadzooks!' said God.

And they flew off to find another
church.

Eeek....
No mammys....

Next, after God had changed back into a man, and changed into a different colo[r]
because God likes difference and can be any sort of person or any color he like[s]
they went into a beautiful big white building with huge steps and fountains
outside. Everyone was very well dressed and looked exactly like each other.

'Everyone is *white!*' whispered God to Stardrop. 'Where are all my black and brown people and all my people of different colors?'
'They don't have them here,' answered Chester.
'Gadzooks!' said God.

And they flew off to find another church.

Next they went to a church on a very pretty hill where everyone was jumping up and down and shouting lots of great things about God.

YEA YEA YEA!

WOW –
BACKWARDS!

'Why don't they sit still and just listen to each
other?' whispered God to Stardrop.
'Because they want to make sure that *You* can
hear *them*,' answered Chester.
'Gadzooks!' said God.

And they flew off to find another church.

And then they all went to a church where a man called a preacher stood up and talked and talked and talked and talked about how everyone had to be good and not make God mad.

'When is he going to tell them how much I love them?' whispered God.
'When they stop being naughty,' answered Chester.
'Gadzooks!' said God.

By this time they were all tired.
And off they flew...

...to THE PARK!

hildren were playing. Old people were sitting peacefully and quietly. Young
eople were smiling and laughing and holding hands. Birds were singing. Flowers
ere dancing. Even the fish were jumping up and down. People were sitting
gether and sharing picnics.

'This,' whispered God, 'is the best church of all.'

'And YOU made it!' answered Chester with an excited squeak.

'Ssssssshhhh!' whispered God.

'It's a secret!'